BOATS
for
BEDTIME

by
Olga Litowinsky

Illustrated by
Melanie Hope Greenberg

Clarion Books • New York

Clarion Books
a Houghton Mifflin Company imprint
215 Park Avenue South, New York, NY 10003
Text copyright © 1999 by Olga Litowinsky
Illustrations copyright © 1999 by Melanie Hope Greenberg

Text is 28-point Helvetica Rounded
Illustrations executed in Turner Design Colour on Lanaquarelle paper
All rights reserved.

For information about permission to reproduce selections from this book, write to Permissions,
Houghton Mifflin Company, 215 Park Avenue South, New York, NY 10003.

4516   Printed in Singapore

Library of Congress Cataloging-in-Publication Data

Litowinsky, Olga.
Boats for bedtime / by Olga Litowinsky ; illustrated by Melanie Hope Greenberg.
p. cm.
ISBN 0-395-89128-0
[1. A child imagines all kinds of boats in all kinds of places as he settles down to sleep.
2. Boats and boating—Fiction. 3. Bedtime—Fiction.] I. Greenberg, Melanie Hope, ill. II. Title.
PZ7.L698Bo 1999
[E]—dc21   98-26158
CIP
AC

TWP 10 9 8 7 6 5 4 3 2 1

For Zachary

—O. L.

For my mother, in loving memory

—M. H. G.

Boats in the bathtub

Big boats

Little boats

Boats in all sizes

Snug boats

Tugboats

Boats in the harbor

Boats on the sea

Tankers

Trawlers

Liners

Lifeboats

Freighters

Ferry boats

Boats working hard

Night and day

Boats for pleasure everywhere

Sailboats

Rowboats

Kayaks

Canoes

Boats on the lake

Boats on the beach

Boats on the highway

Boats on boats!

Out of water

In the water

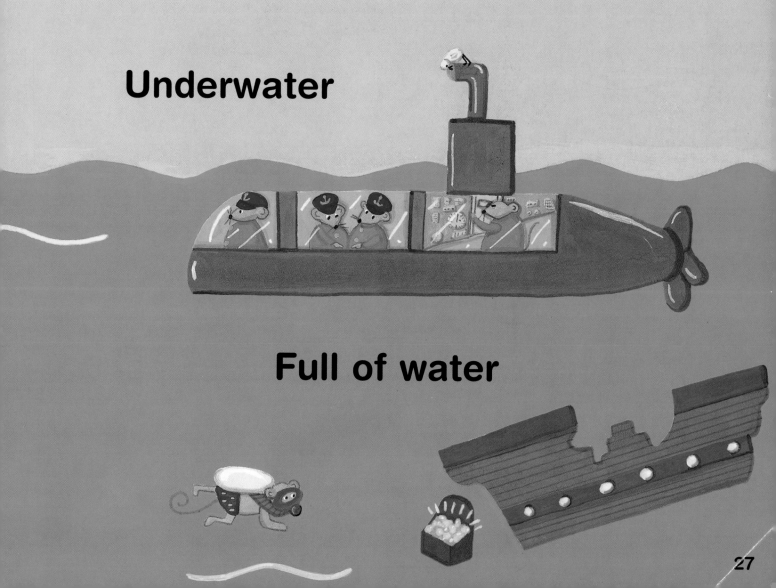

Underwater

Full of water

Boats in the sky

Sail among the stars

Play around the moon

All night long